Y0-BGH-429

Big Dreams

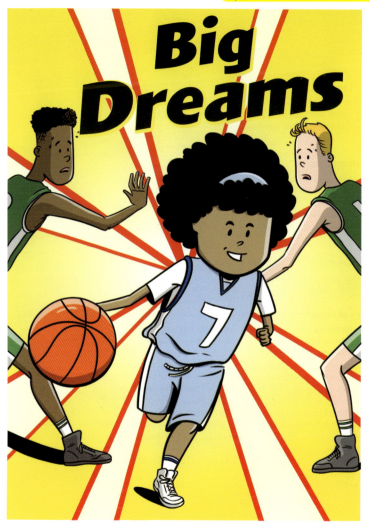

By Joe Rhatigan
Illustrated by Joseph McDermott

Consultant

Kristin Risdahl, M.S.Ed.
K–12 Social Studies Instructional Facilitator
Knox County Schools, Tennessee

Publishing Credits

Rachelle Cracchiolo, M.S.Ed., *Publisher*
Emily R. Smith, M.A.Ed., *VP of Content Development*
Véronique Bos, *Creative Director*
Dani Neiley, *Associate Editor*
Kevin Pham, *Graphic Designer*

Image Credits

Illustrated by Joseph McDermott

Library of Congress Cataloging-in-Publication Data

Names: Rhatigan, Joe, author. | McDermott, Joseph, illustrator.
Title: Big dreams / by Joe Rhatigan ; illustrated by Joseph McDermott.
Description: Huntington Beach, CA : Teacher Created Materials, [2022] |
  Audience: Grades 2-3. | Summary: "Alex has dreams of becoming a
  basketball star. But as the shortest kid on the team, she's struggling.
  She needs to get tall...fast! Or does she?"-- Provided by publisher.
Identifiers: LCCN 2022005938 (print) | LCCN 2022005939 (ebook) | ISBN
  9781087605456 (paperback) | ISBN 9781087632315 (ebook)
Subjects: LCSH: Readers (Primary) | Basketball players--Juvenile fiction. |
  Basketball players--Comic books, strips, etc. | LCGFT: Readers
  (Publications) | Graphic novels.
Classification: LCC PE1119.2 .R4325 2022 (print) | LCC PE1119.2 (ebook) |
  DDC 428.6/2--dc23/eng/20220211
LC record available at https://lccn.loc.gov/2022005938
LC ebook record available at https://lccn.loc.gov/2022005939

TCM Teacher Created Materials

5482 Argosy Avenue
Huntington Beach, CA 92649
www.tcmpub.com

ISBN 978-1-0876-0545-6

© 2023 Teacher Created Materials, Inc.
Printed in Malaysia.THU001.50393
This book may not be reproduced or distributed in any way without prior written consent from the publisher.

Table of Contents

Chapter One

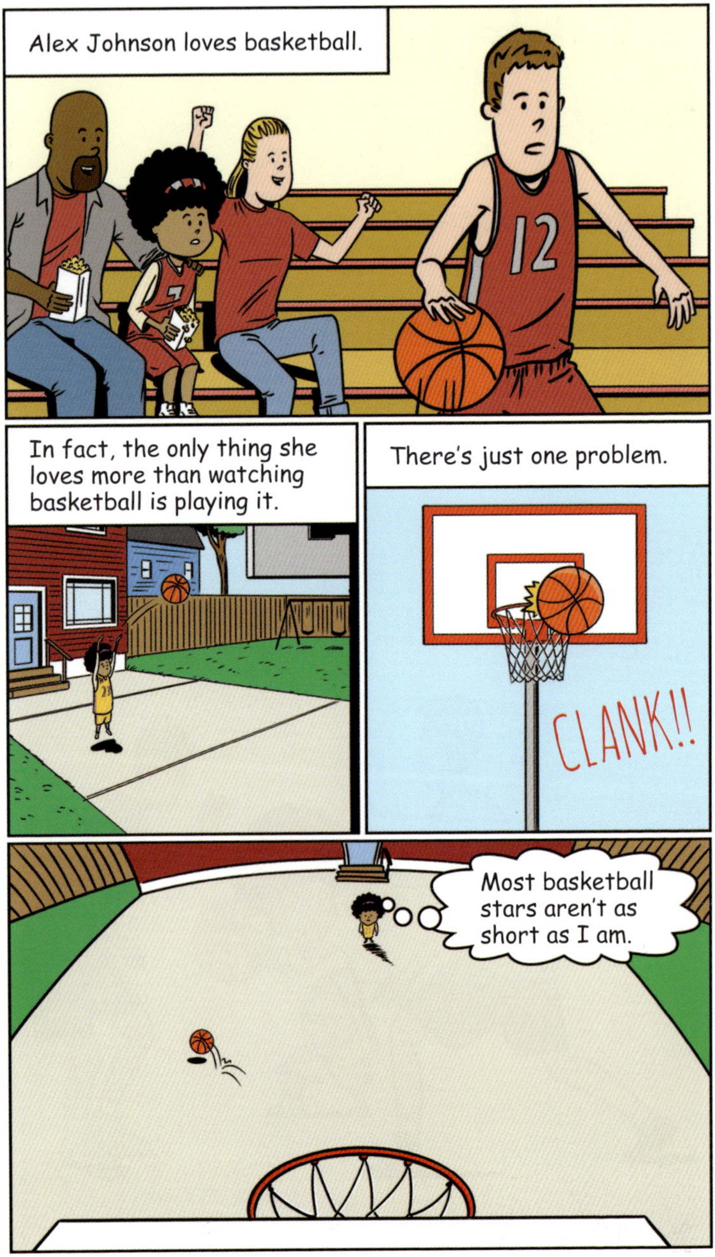
Alex Johnson loves basketball.
12
In fact, the only thing she loves more than watching basketball is playing it.
There's just one problem.
CLANK!!
Most basketball stars aren't as short as I am.

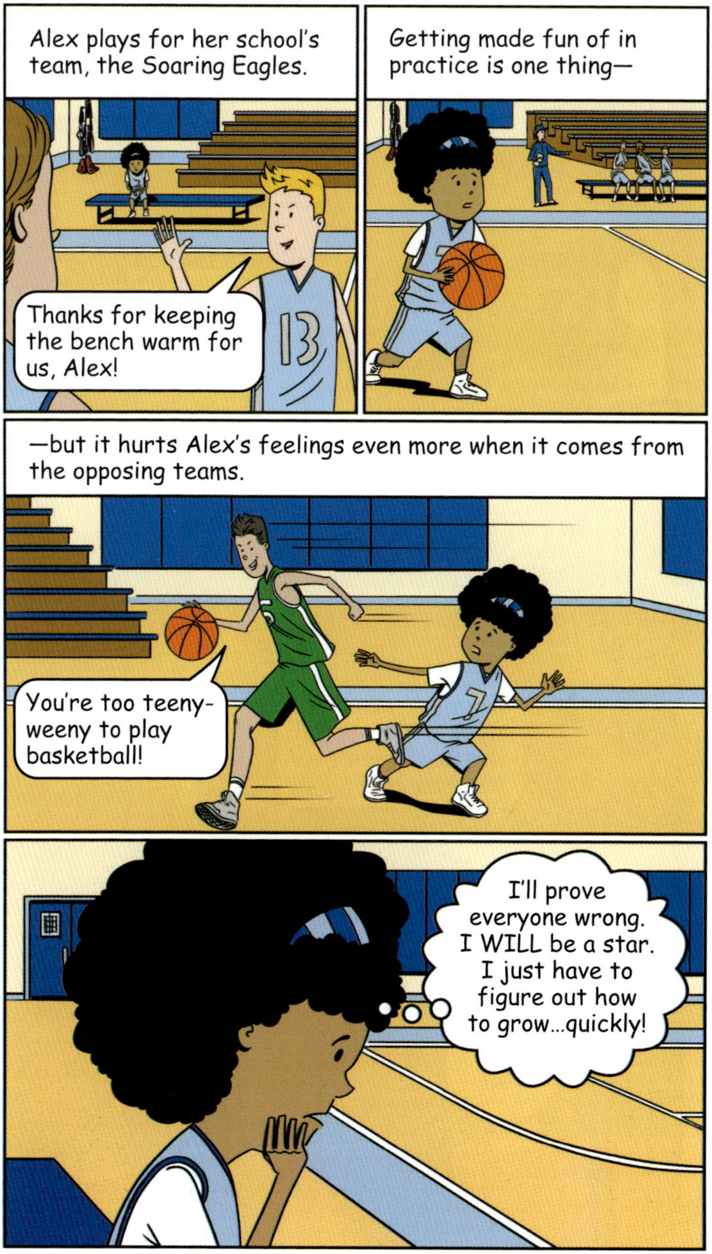
Alex plays for her school's team, the Soaring Eagles.
Thanks for keeping the bench warm for us, Alex!
Getting made fun of in practice is one thing—
—but it hurts Alex's feelings even more when it comes from the opposing teams.
You're too teeny-weeny to play basketball!
I'll prove everyone wrong. I WILL be a star. I just have to figure out how to grow...quickly!

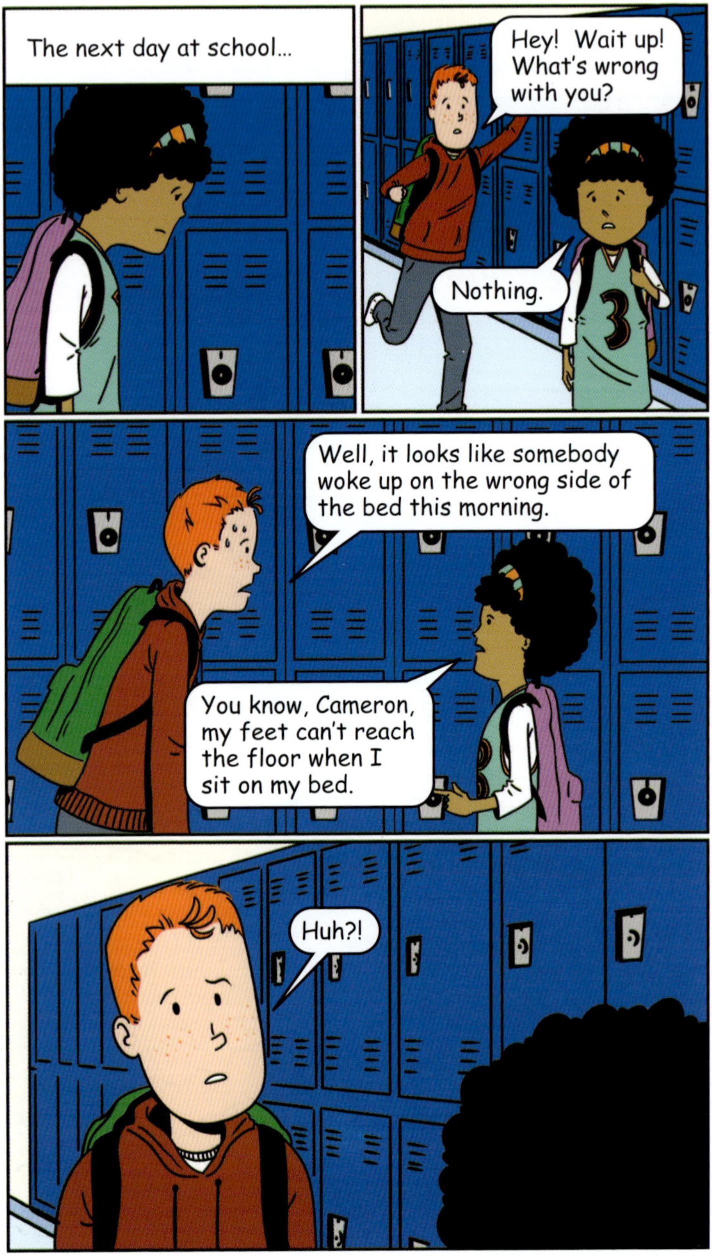
The next day at school...
Hey! Wait up! What's wrong with you?
Nothing.
Well, it looks like somebody woke up on the wrong side of the bed this morning.
You know, Cameron, my feet can't reach the floor when I sit on my bed.
Huh?!

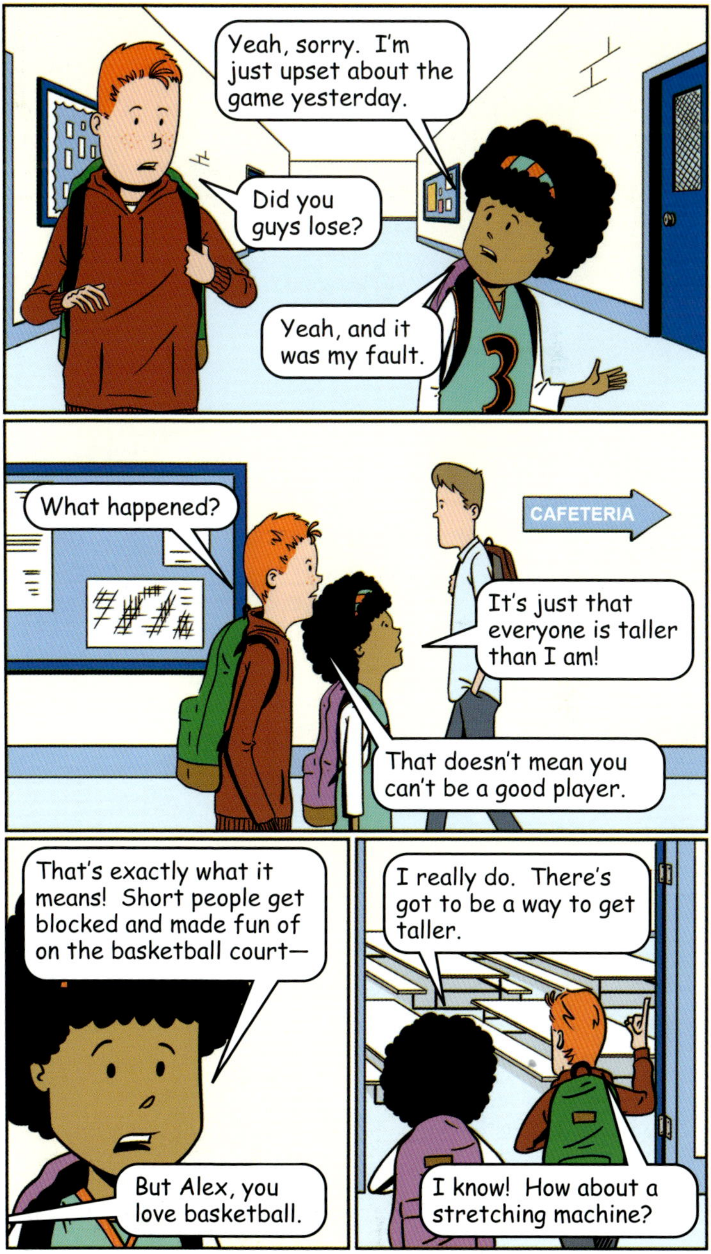
Yeah, sorry. I'm just upset about the game yesterday.
Did you guys lose?
Yeah, and it was my fault.
What happened?
CAFETERIA
It's just that everyone is taller than I am!
That doesn't mean you can't be a good player.
That's exactly what it means! Short people get blocked and made fun of on the basketball court—
But Alex, you love basketball.
I really do. There's got to be a way to get taller.
I know! How about a stretching machine?

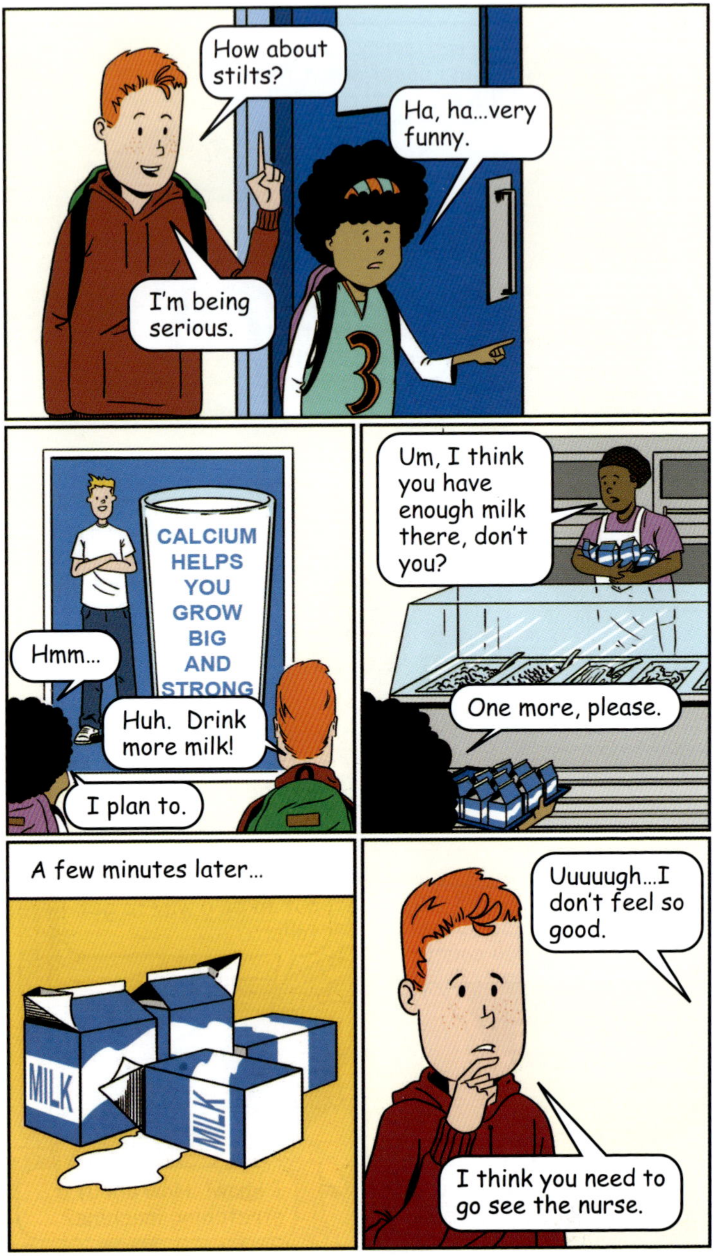
How about stilts?
Ha, ha...very funny.
I'm being serious.
CALCIUM HELPS YOU GROW BIG AND STRONG
Hmm...
Huh. Drink more milk!
I plan to.
Um, I think you have enough milk there, don't you?
One more, please.
A few minutes later...
MILK
MILK
Uuuuugh...I don't feel so good.
I think you need to go see the nurse.

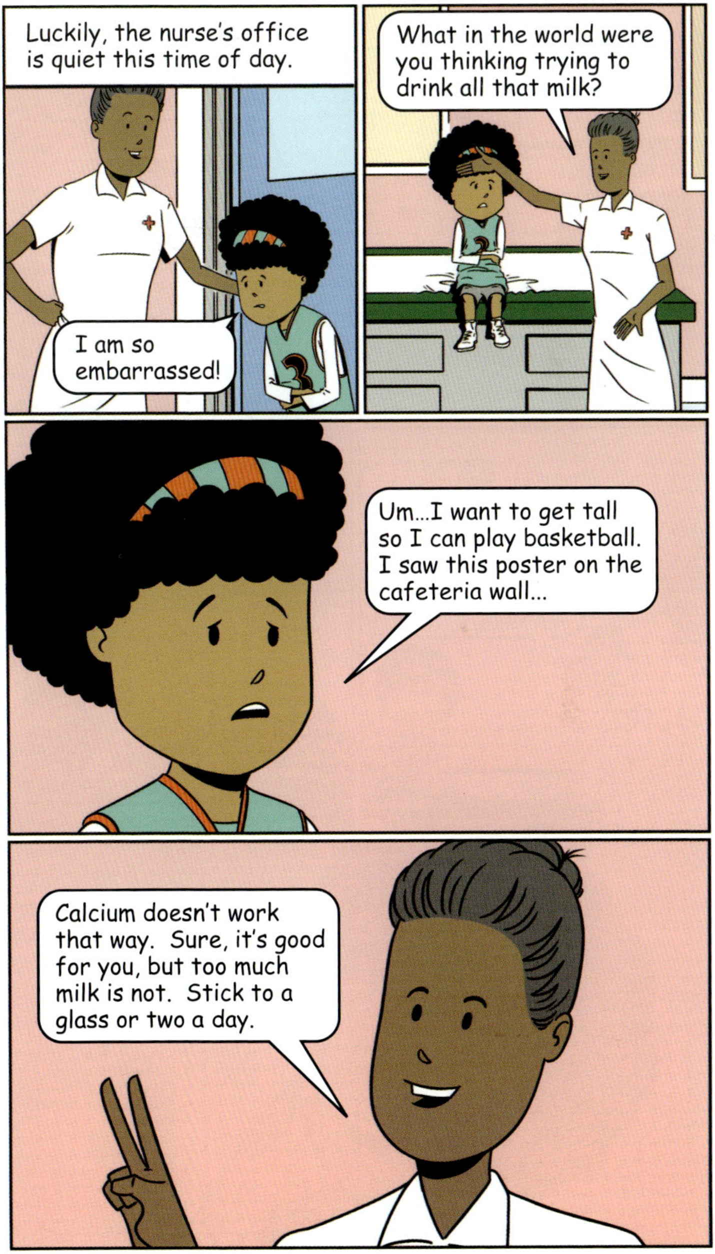
Luckily, the nurse's office is quiet this time of day.
I am so embarrassed!
What in the world were you thinking trying to drink all that milk?
Um...I want to get tall so I can play basketball. I saw this poster on the cafeteria wall...
Calcium doesn't work that way. Sure, it's good for you, but too much milk is not. Stick to a glass or two a day.

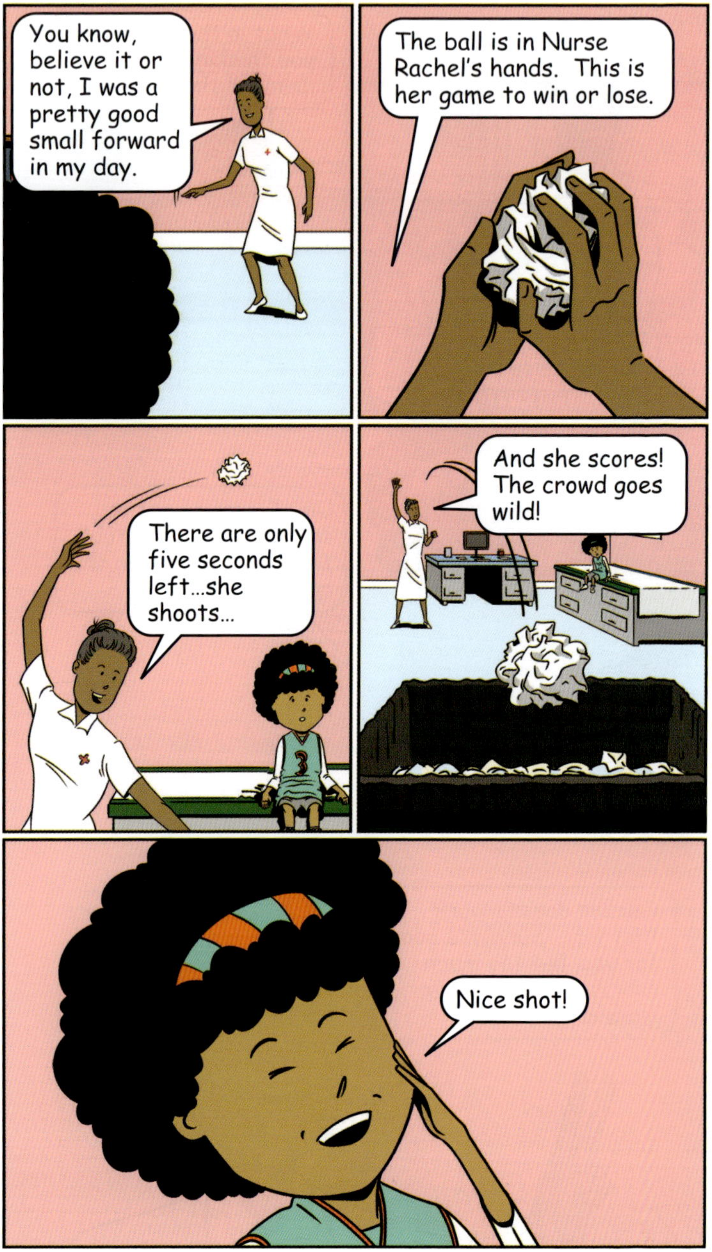
You know, believe it or not, I was a pretty good small forward in my day.
The ball is in Nurse Rachel's hands. This is her game to win or lose.
There are only five seconds left...she shoots...
And she scores! The crowd goes wild!
Nice shot!

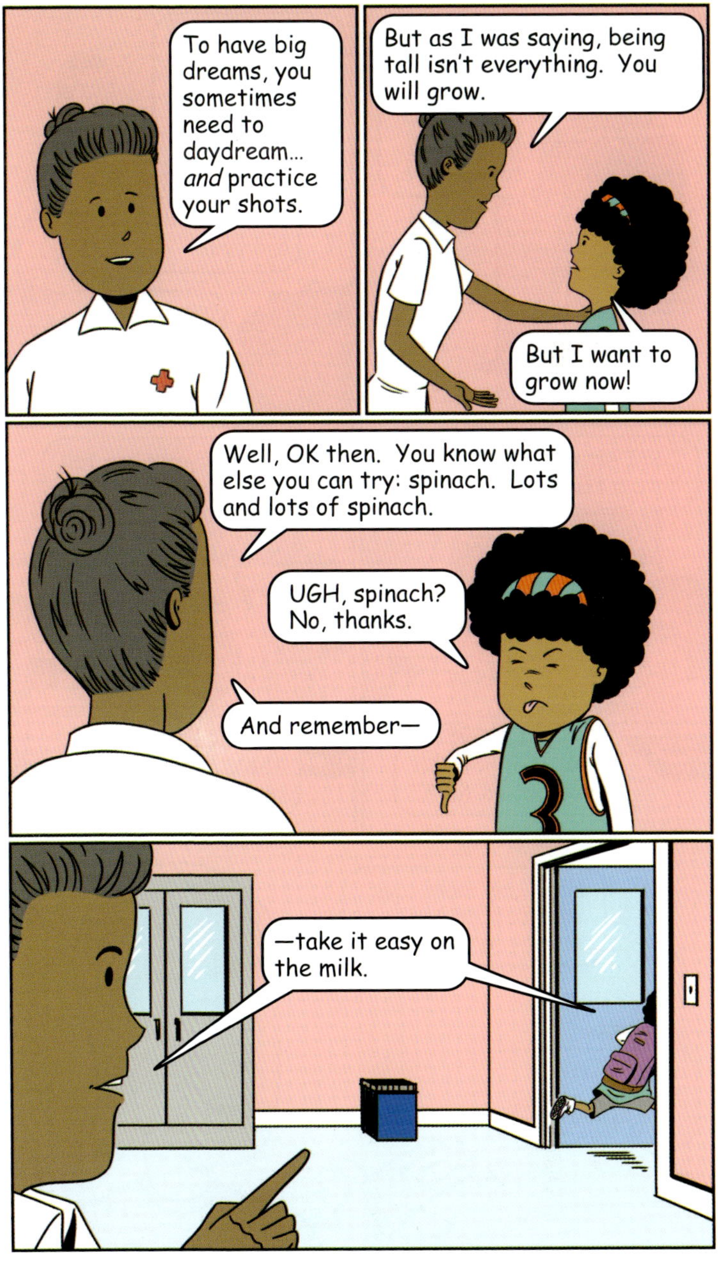
To have big dreams, you sometimes need to daydream... *and* practice your shots.
But as I was saying, being tall isn't everything. You will grow.
But I want to grow now!
Well, OK then. You know what else you can try: spinach. Lots and lots of spinach.
UGH, spinach? No, thanks.
And remember—
—take it easy on the milk.

Chapter Two

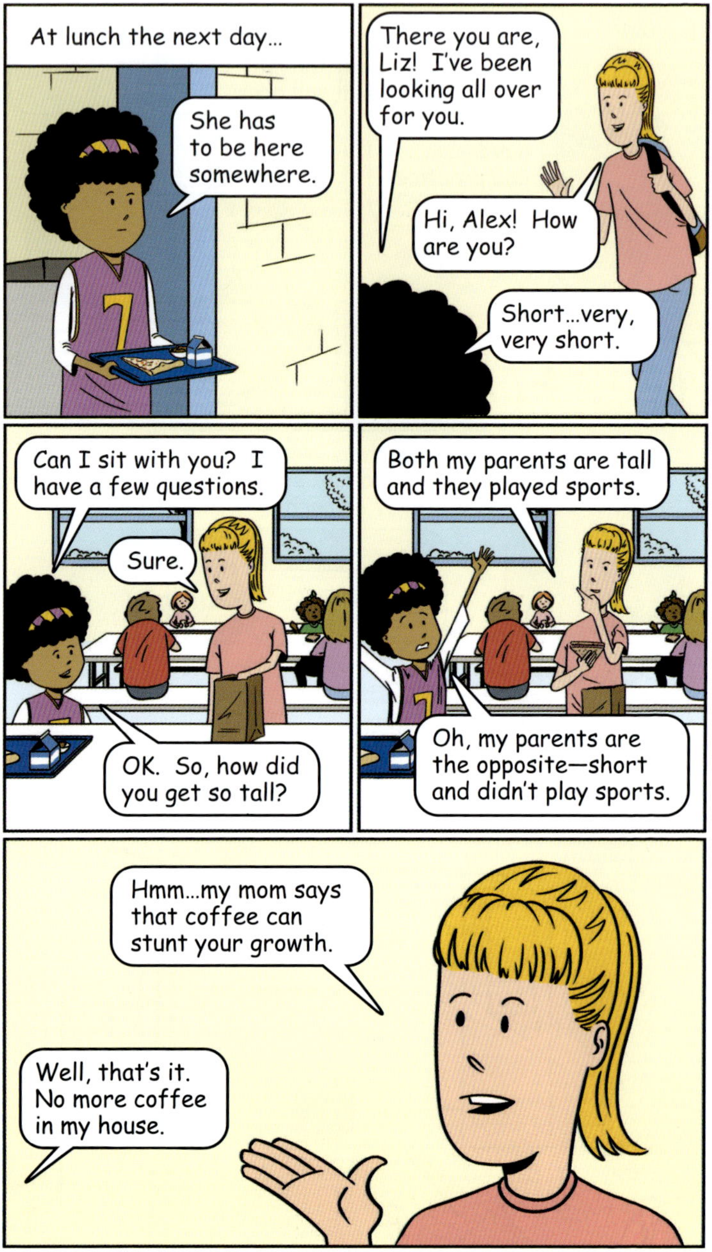
At lunch the next day...
She has to be here somewhere.
There you are, Liz! I've been looking all over for you.
Hi, Alex! How are you?
Short...very, very short.
Can I sit with you? I have a few questions.
Sure.
OK. So, how did you get so tall?
Both my parents are tall and they played sports.
Oh, my parents are the opposite—short and didn't play sports.
Hmm...my mom says that coffee can stunt your growth.
Well, that's it. No more coffee in my house.

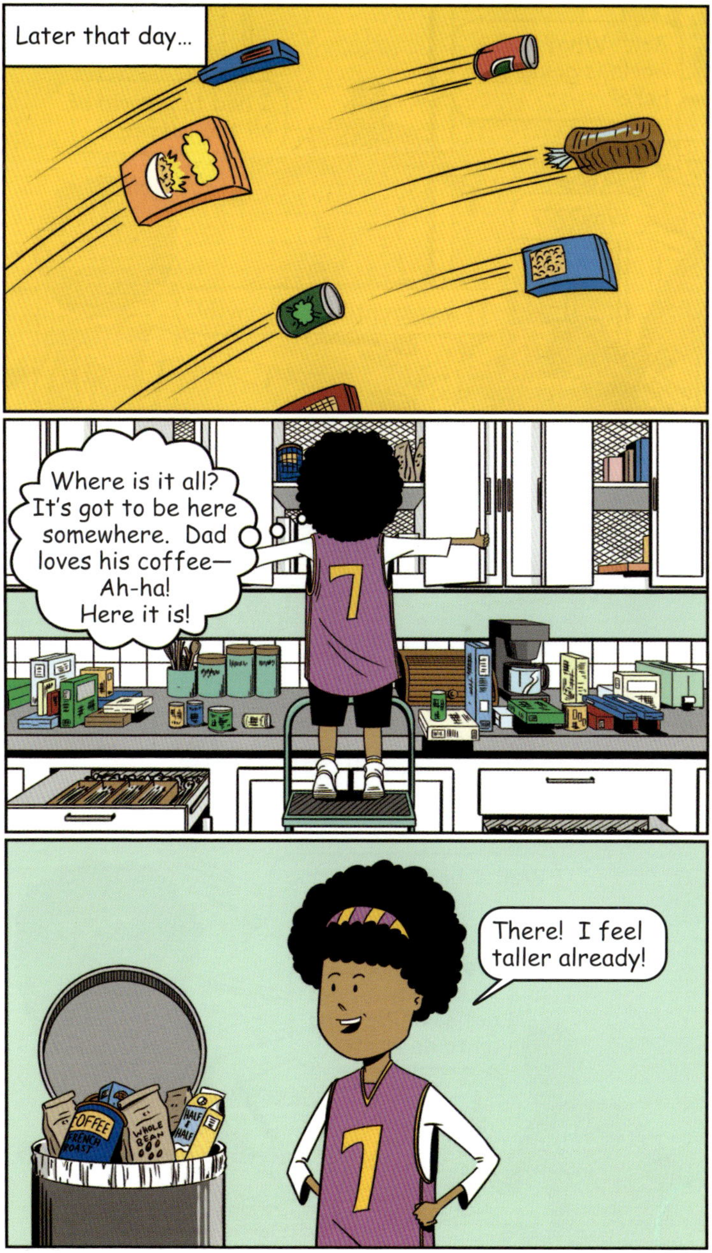
Later that day...
Where is it all? It's got to be here somewhere. Dad loves his coffee— Ah-ha! Here it is!
COFFEE
FRENCH ROAST
WHOLE BEAN
HALF & HALF
There! I feel taller already!

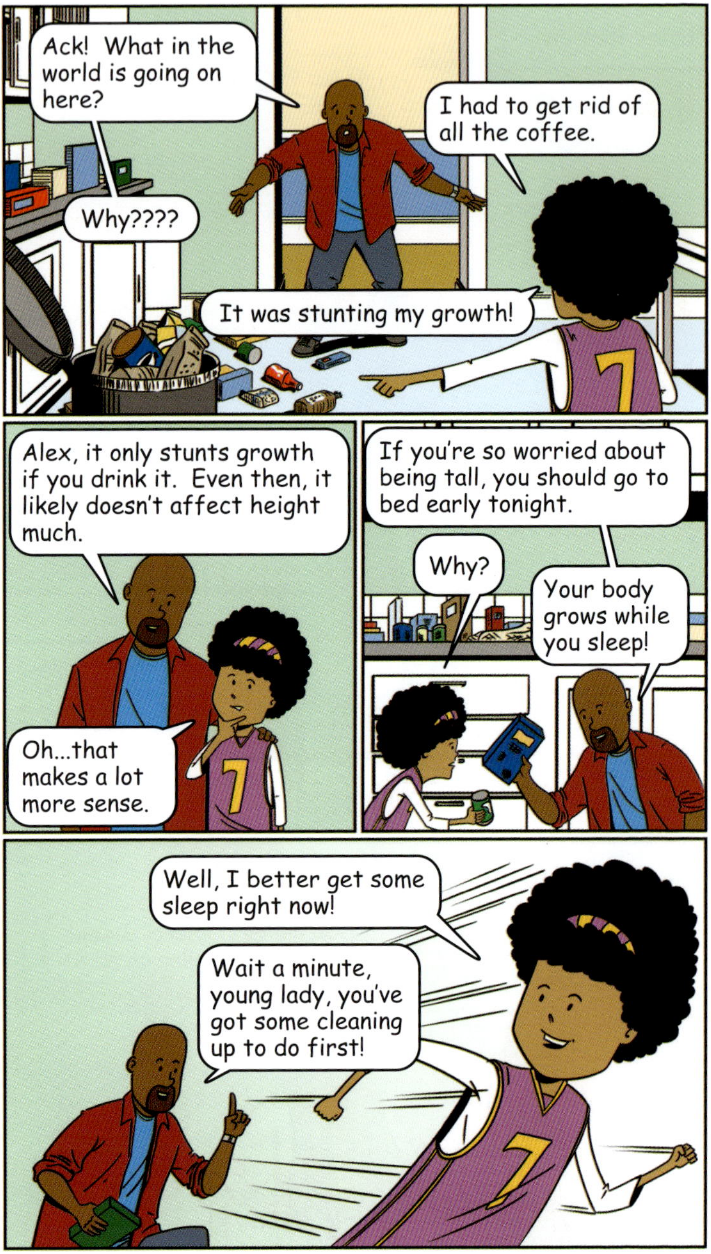
Ack! What in the world is going on here?
Why????
I had to get rid of all the coffee.
It was stunting my growth!
Alex, it only stunts growth if you drink it. Even then, it likely doesn't affect height much.
Oh...that makes a lot more sense.
If you're so worried about being tall, you should go to bed early tonight.
Why?
Your body grows while you sleep!
Well, I better get some sleep right now!
Wait a minute, young lady, you've got some cleaning up to do first!

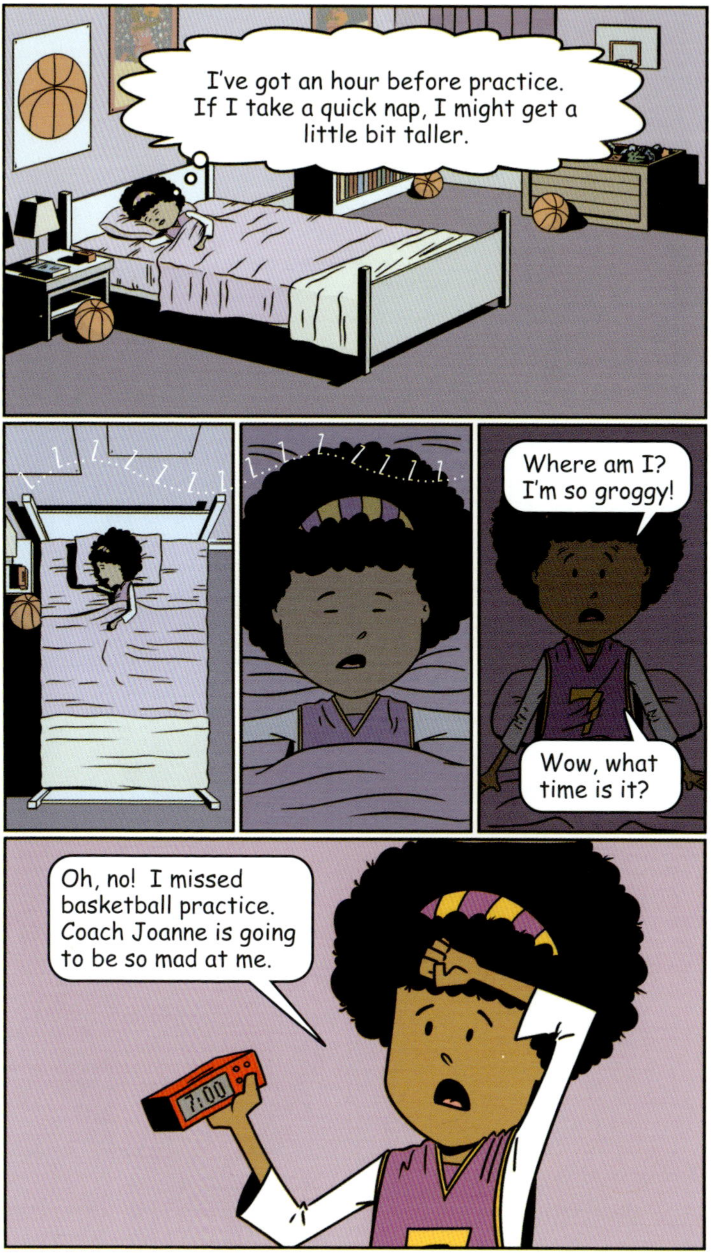
I've got an hour before practice. If I take a quick nap, I might get a little bit taller.
Where am I? I'm so groggy!
Wow, what time is it?
Oh, no! I missed basketball practice. Coach Joanne is going to be so mad at me.
7:00

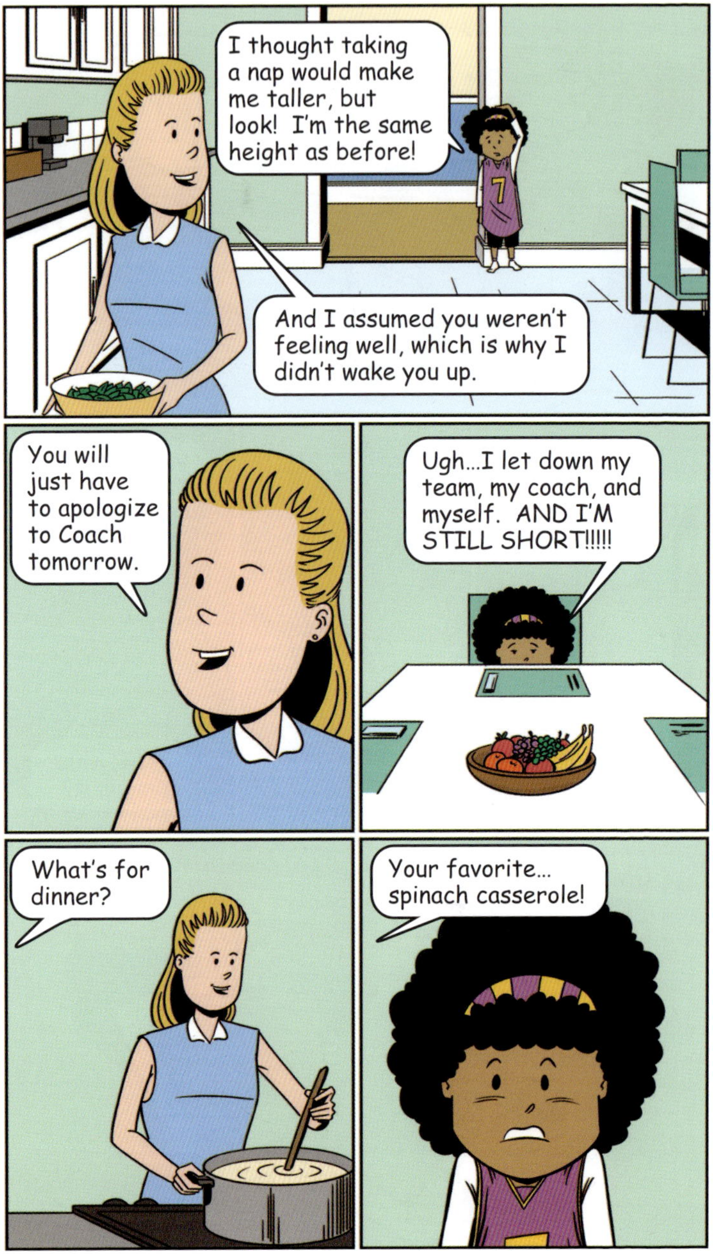
I thought taking a nap would make me taller, but look! I'm the same height as before!
And I assumed you weren't feeling well, which is why I didn't wake you up.
You will just have to apologize to Coach tomorrow.
Ugh...I let down my team, my coach, and myself. AND I'M STILL SHORT!!!!!
What's for dinner?
Your favorite... spinach casserole!

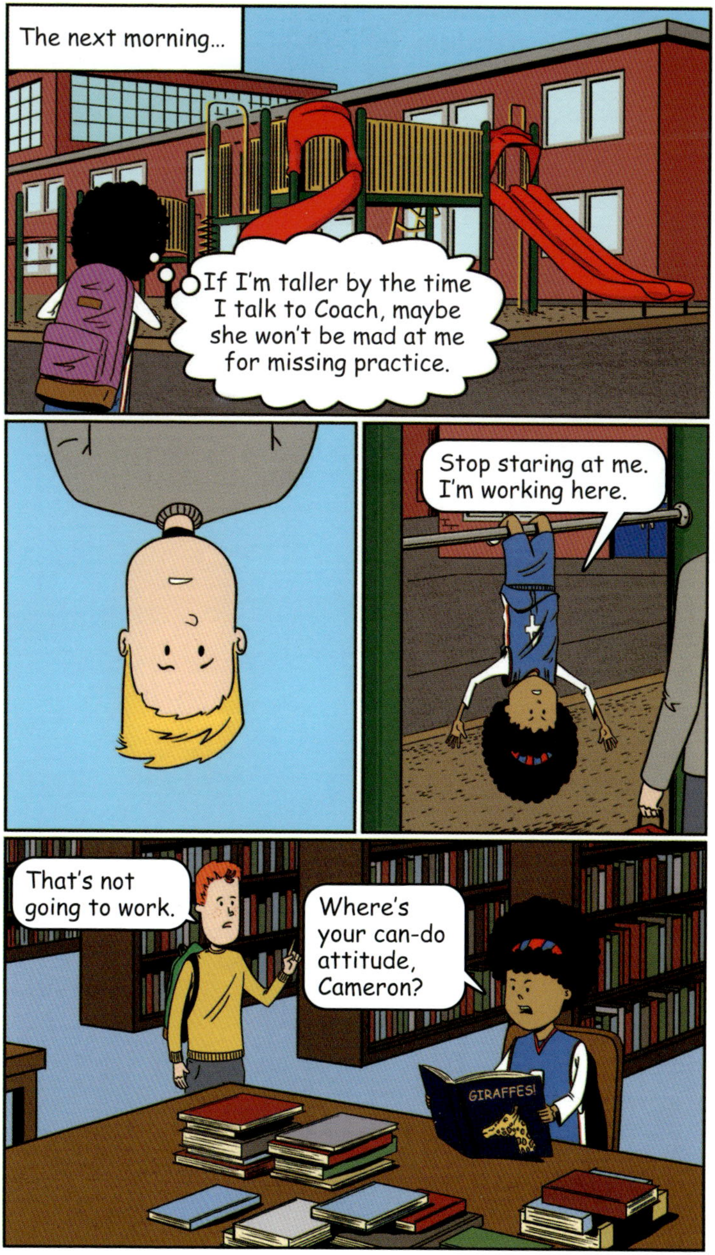
The next morning...
If I'm taller by the time I talk to Coach, maybe she won't be mad at me for missing practice.
Stop staring at me. I'm working here.
That's not going to work.
Where's your can-do attitude, Cameron?
GIRAFFES!

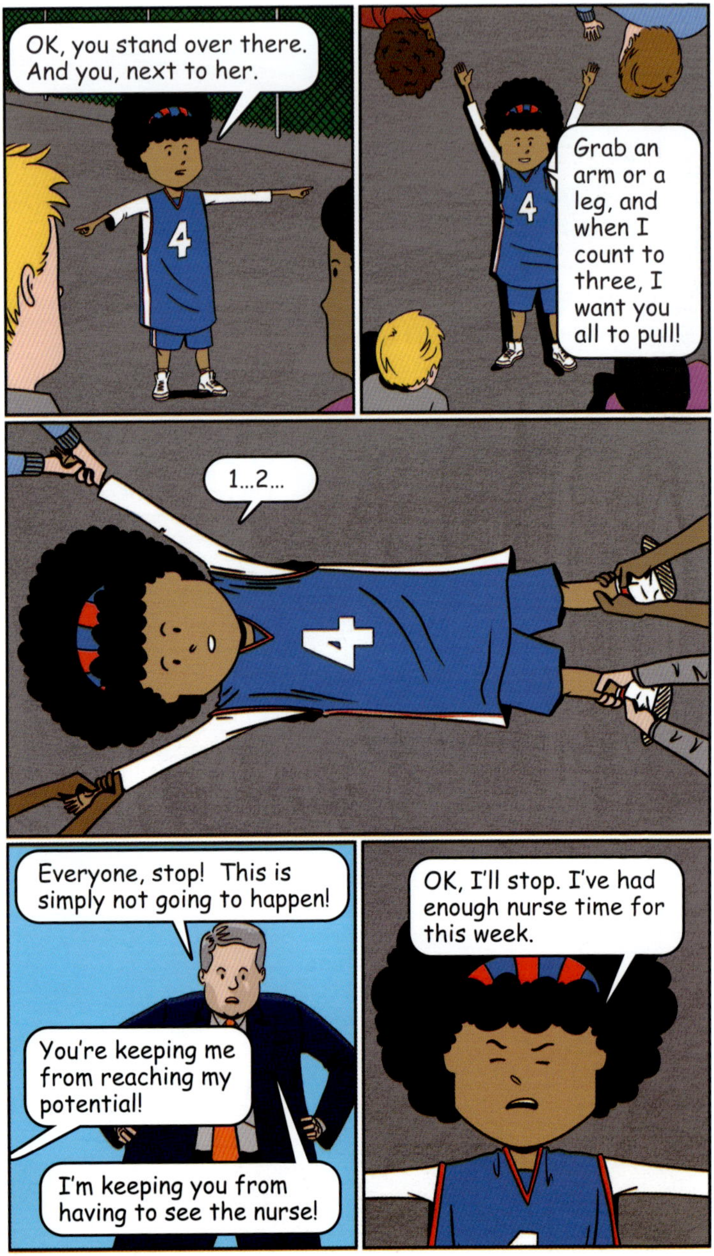
OK, you stand over there. And you, next to her.
Grab an arm or a leg, and when I count to three, I want you all to pull!
1...2...
Everyone, stop! This is simply not going to happen!
You're keeping me from reaching my potential!
I'm keeping you from having to see the nurse!
OK, I'll stop. I've had enough nurse time for this week.

Chapter Three

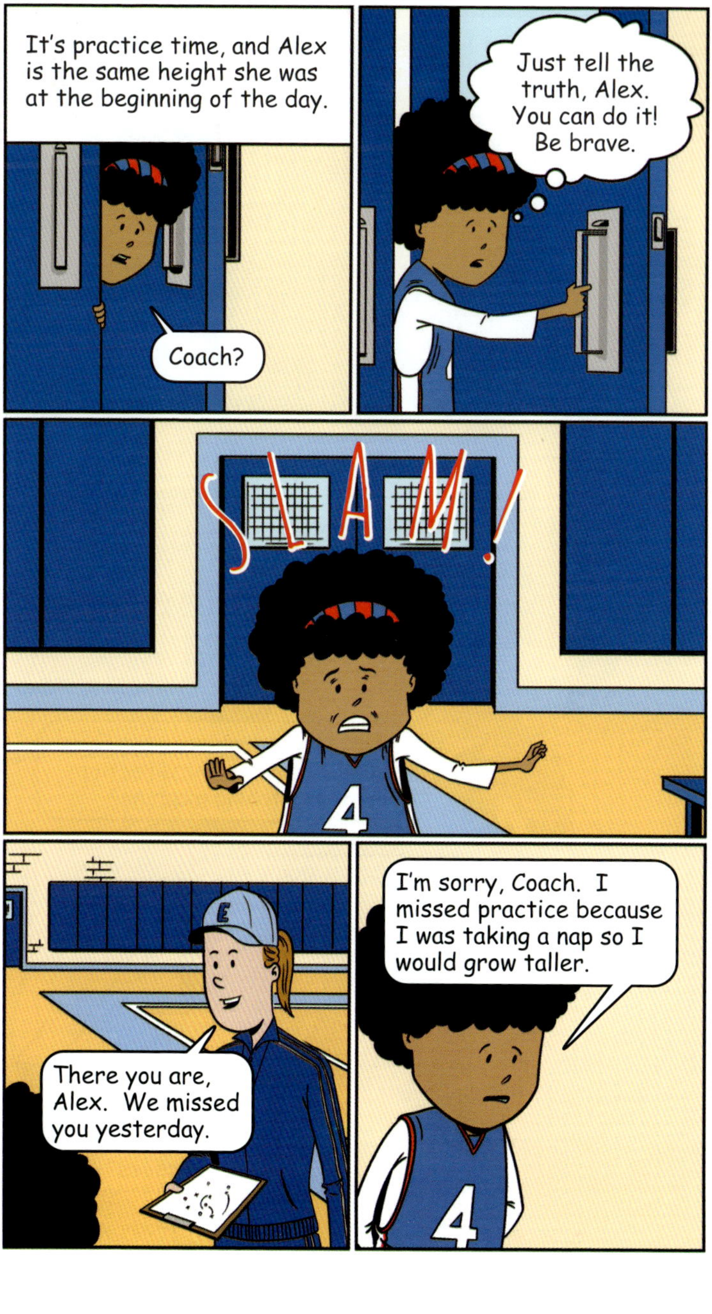

It's practice time, and Alex is the same height she was at the beginning of the day.
Coach?
Just tell the truth, Alex. You can do it! Be brave.
SLAM!
There you are, Alex. We missed you yesterday.
I'm sorry, Coach. I missed practice because I was taking a nap so I would grow taller.

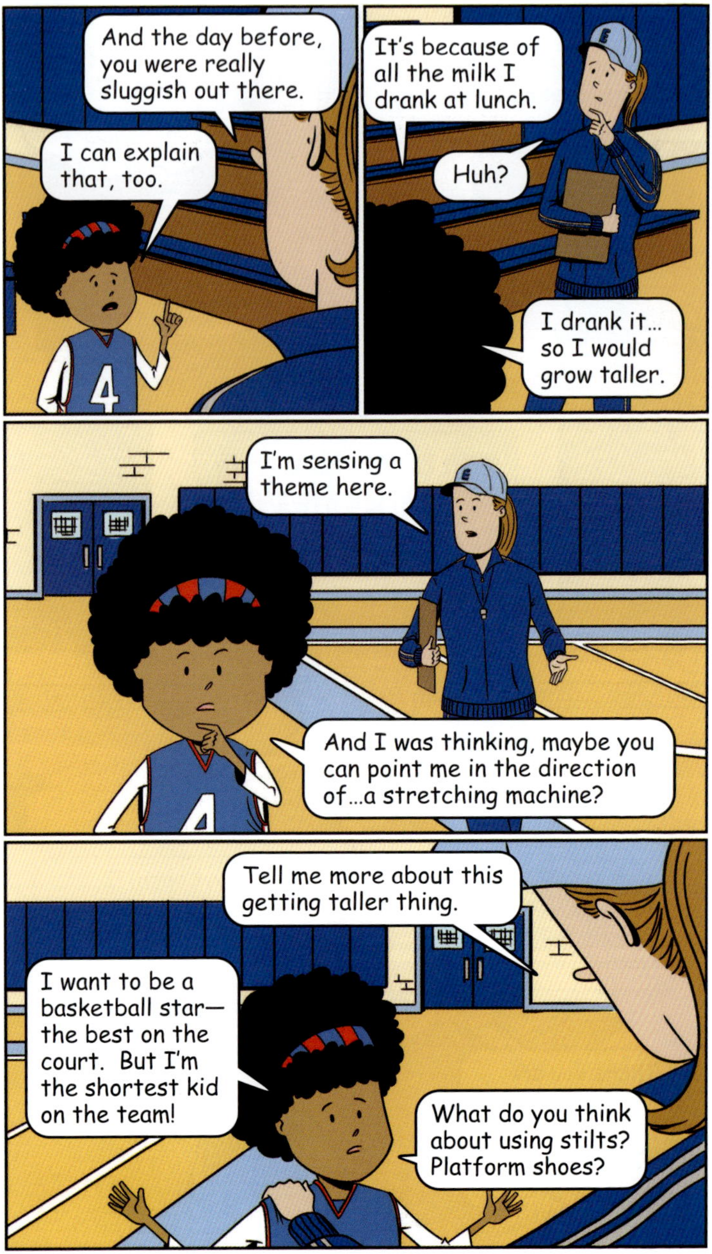
And the day before, you were really sluggish out there.
I can explain that, too.
It's because of all the milk I drank at lunch.
Huh?
I drank it... so I would grow taller.
I'm sensing a theme here.
And I was thinking, maybe you can point me in the direction of...a stretching machine?
Tell me more about this getting taller thing.
I want to be a basketball star—the best on the court. But I'm the shortest kid on the team!
What do you think about using stilts? Platform shoes?

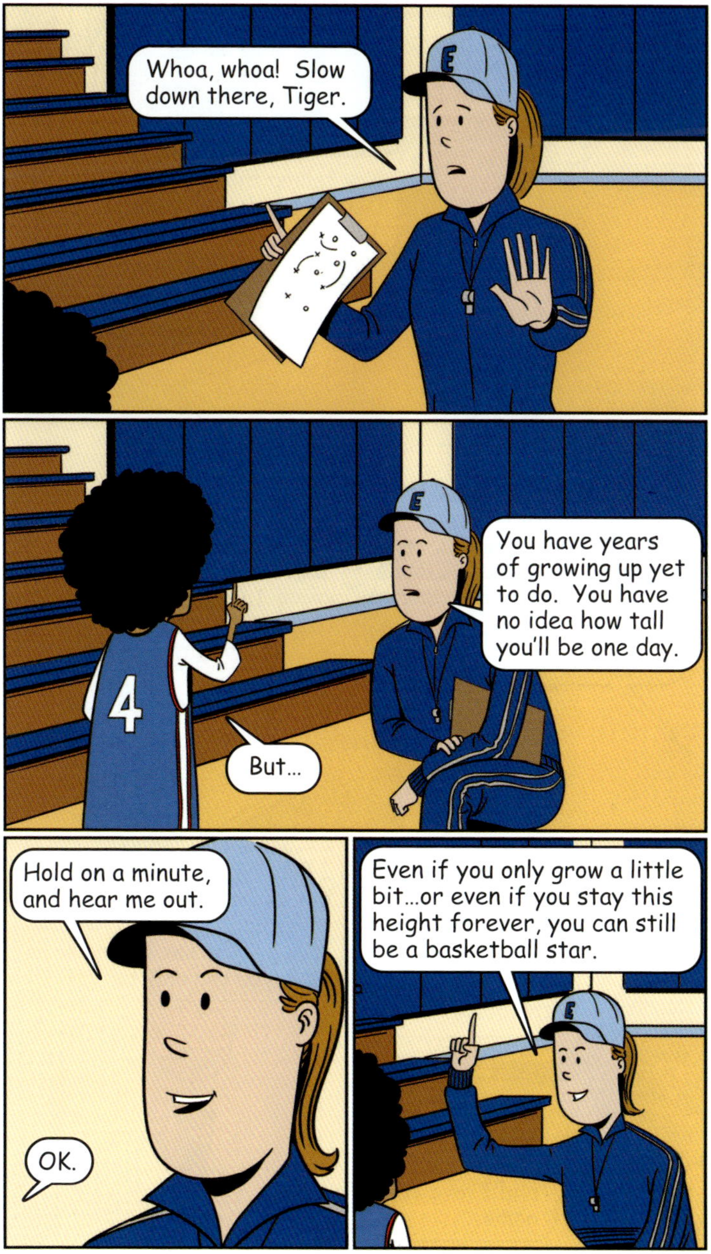

Whoa, whoa! Slow down there, Tiger.
You have years of growing up yet to do. You have no idea how tall you'll be one day.
But...
Hold on a minute, and hear me out.
OK.
Even if you only grow a little bit...or even if you stay this height forever, you can still be a basketball star.

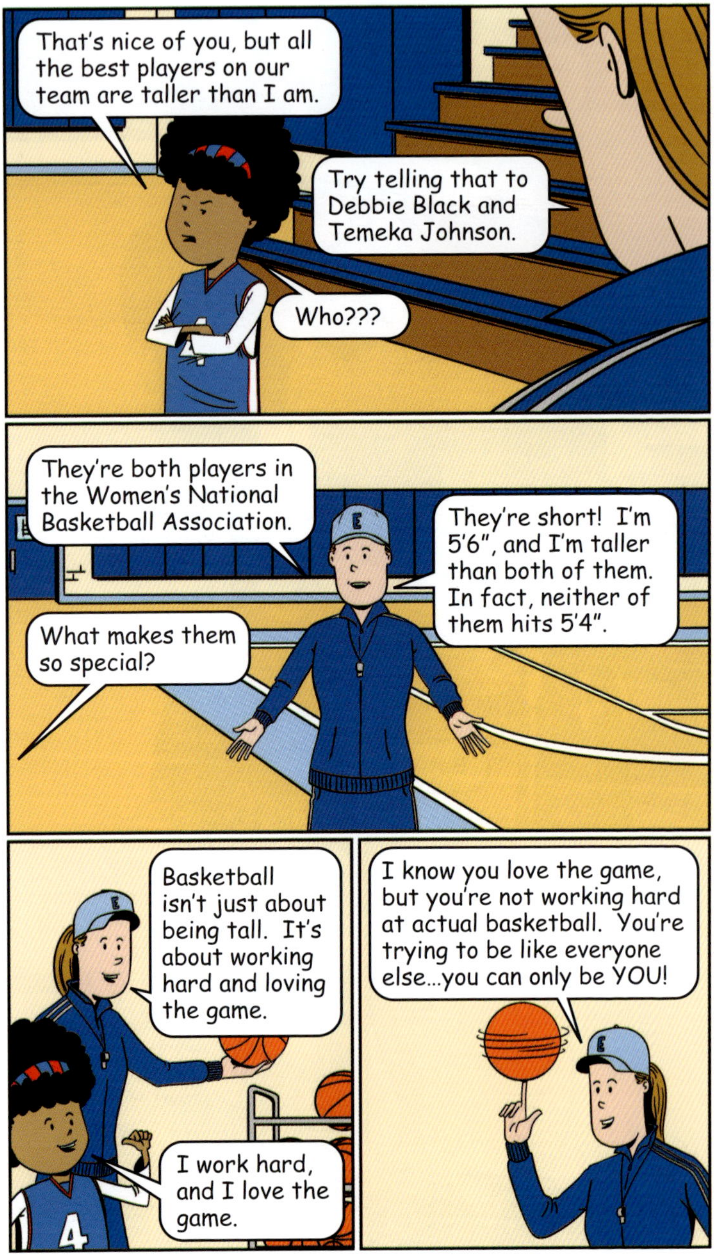

That's nice of you, but all the best players on our team are taller than I am.
Try telling that to Debbie Black and Temeka Johnson.
Who???
They're both players in the Women's National Basketball Association.
What makes them so special?
They're short! I'm 5'6", and I'm taller than both of them. In fact, neither of them hits 5'4".
Basketball isn't just about being tall. It's about working hard and loving the game.
I work hard, and I love the game.
I know you love the game, but you're not working hard at actual basketball. You're trying to be like everyone else...you can only be YOU!

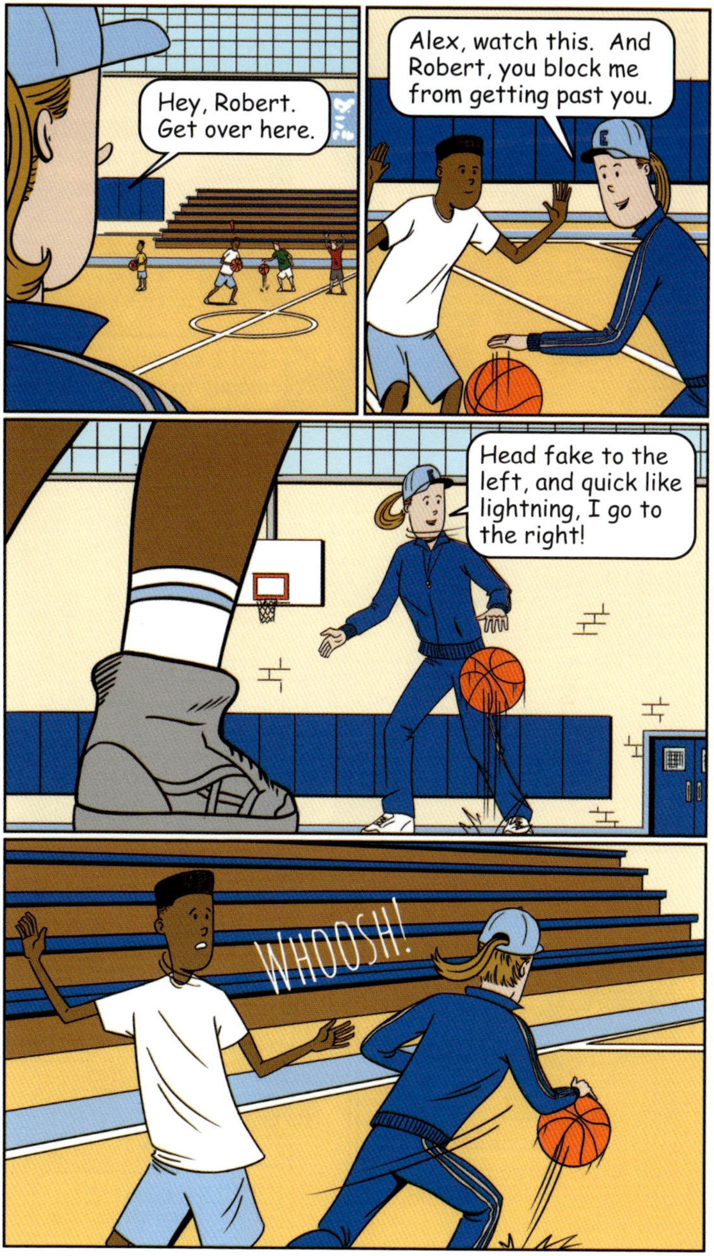
Hey, Robert.
Get over here.
Alex, watch this. And Robert, you block me from getting past you.
Head fake to the left, and quick like lightning, I go to the right!
WHOOSH!

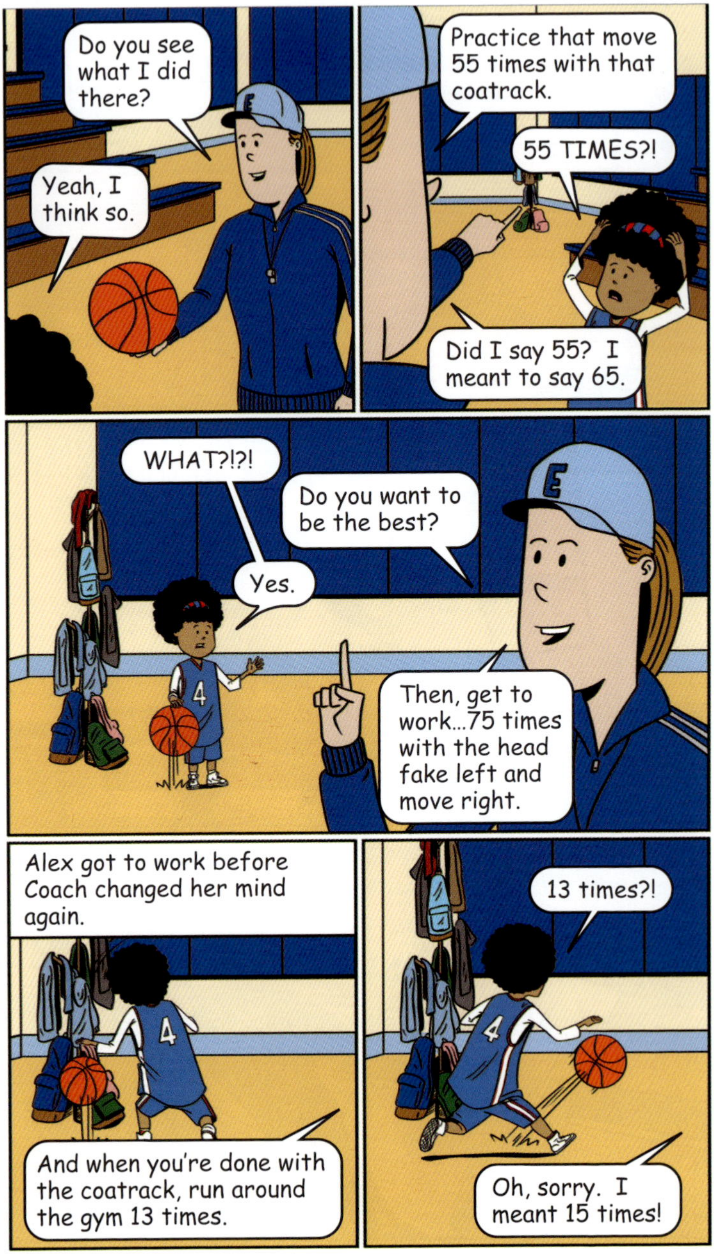
Do you see what I did there?
Yeah, I think so.
Practice that move 55 times with that coatrack.
55 TIMES?!
Did I say 55? I meant to say 65.
WHAT?!?!
Do you want to be the best?
Yes.
Then, get to work...75 times with the head fake left and move right.
Alex got to work before Coach changed her mind again.
And when you're done with the coatrack, run around the gym 13 times.
13 times?!
Oh, sorry. I meant 15 times!

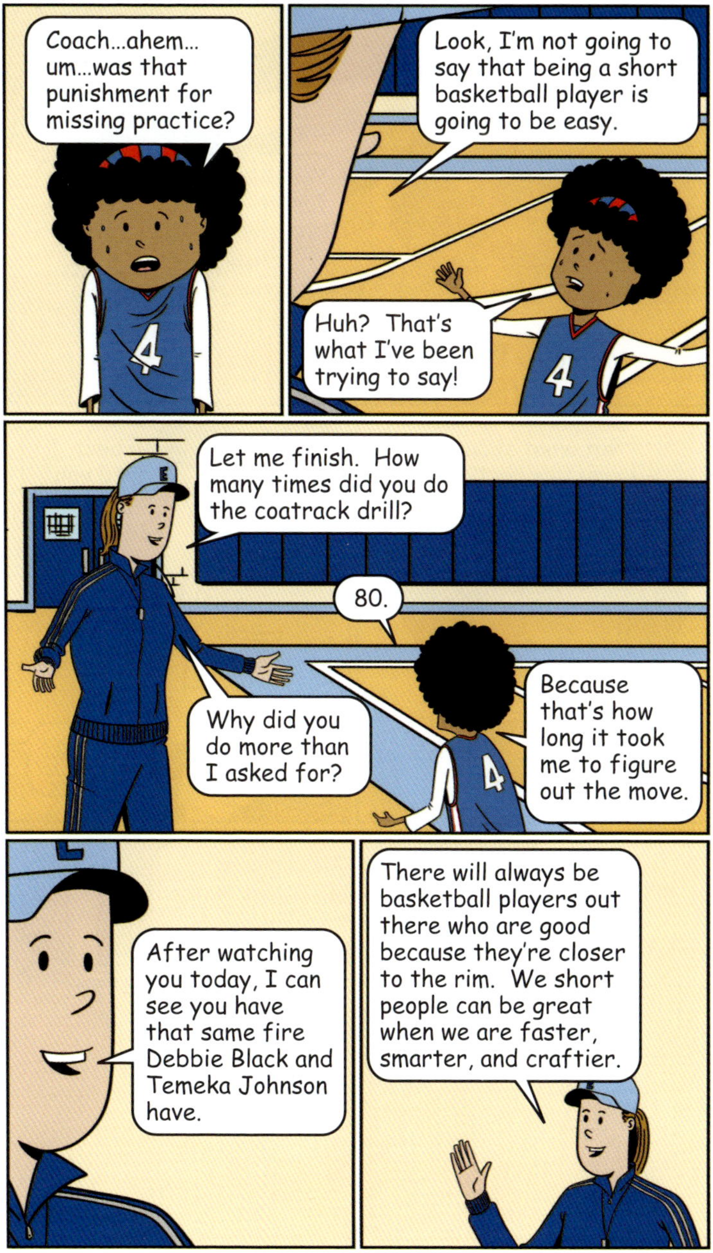
Coach...ahem... um...was that punishment for missing practice?
Look, I'm not going to say that being a short basketball player is going to be easy.
Huh? That's what I've been trying to say!
Let me finish. How many times did you do the coatrack drill?
80.
Why did you do more than I asked for?
Because that's how long it took me to figure out the move.
After watching you today, I can see you have that same fire Debbie Black and Temeka Johnson have.
There will always be basketball players out there who are good because they're closer to the rim. We short people can be great when we are faster, smarter, and craftier.

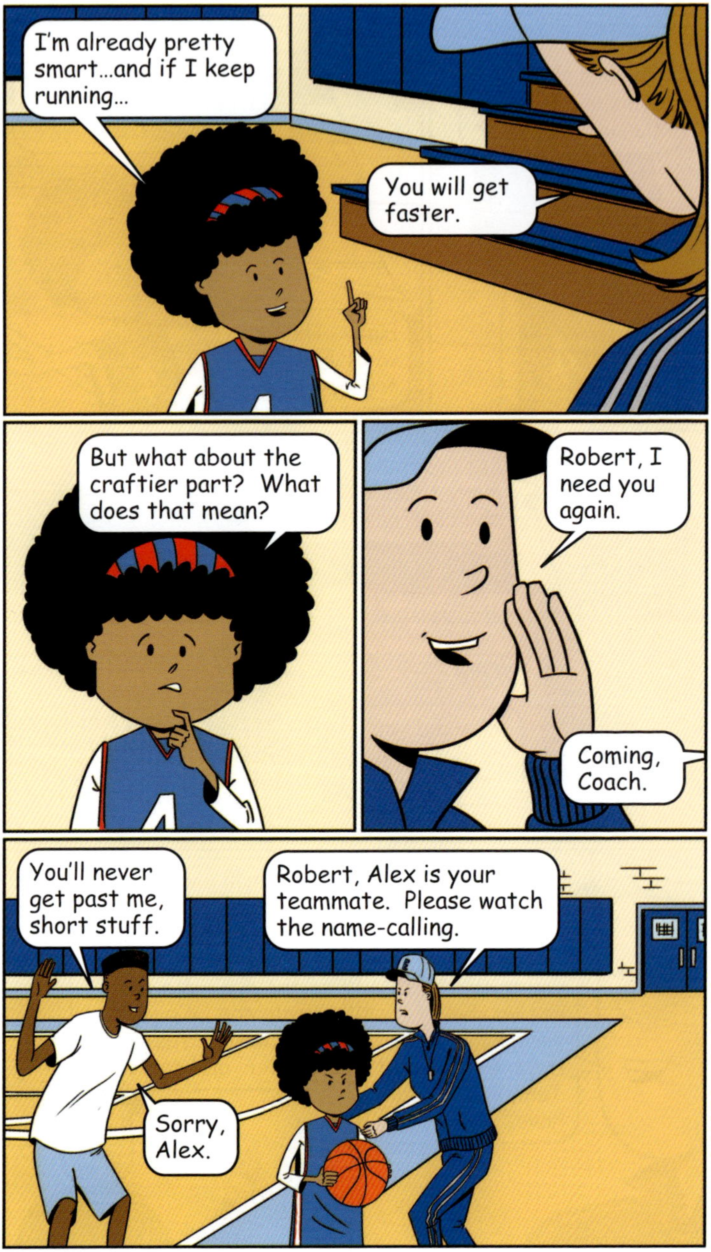
I'm already pretty smart…and if I keep running…
You will get faster.
But what about the craftier part? What does that mean?
Robert, I need you again.
Coming, Coach.
You'll never get past me, short stuff.
Robert, Alex is your teammate. Please watch the name-calling.
Sorry, Alex.

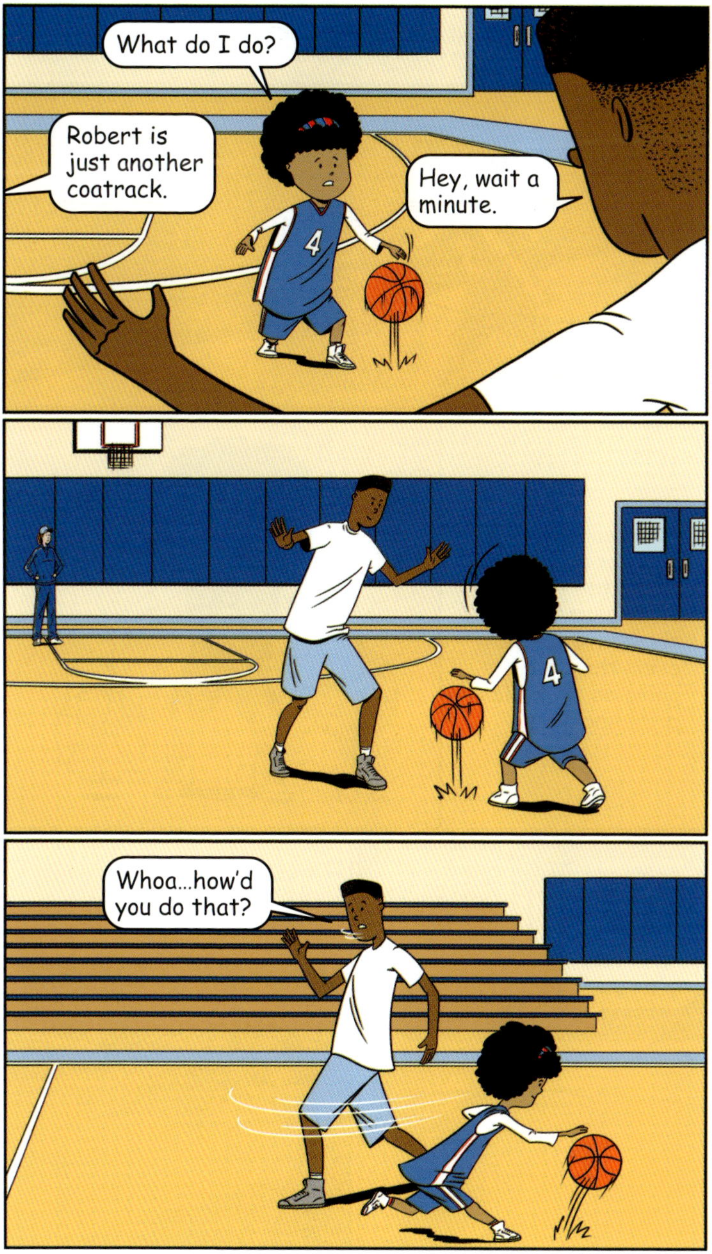
What do I do?
Robert is just another coatrack.
Hey, wait a minute.
Whoa...how'd you do that?

Chapter Four

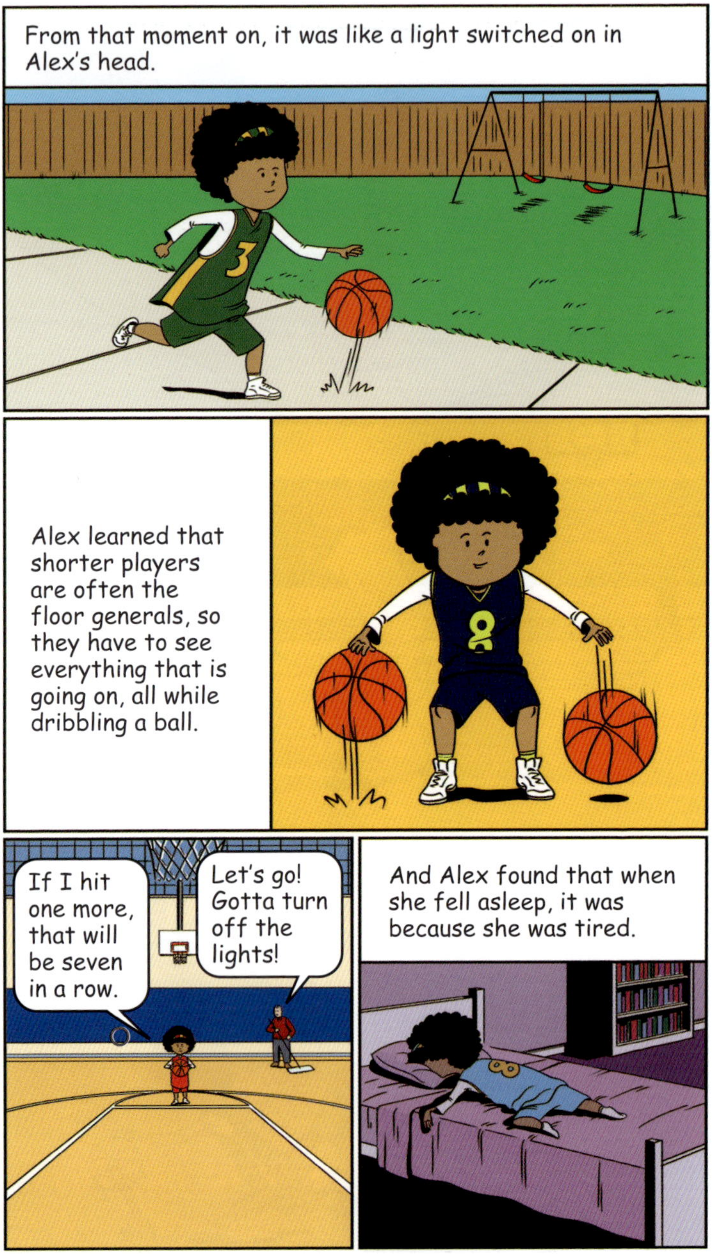
From that moment on, it was like a light switched on in Alex's head.
Alex learned that shorter players are often the floor generals, so they have to see everything that is going on, all while dribbling a ball.
If I hit one more, that will be seven in a row.
Let's go! Gotta turn off the lights!
And Alex found that when she fell asleep, it was because she was tired.

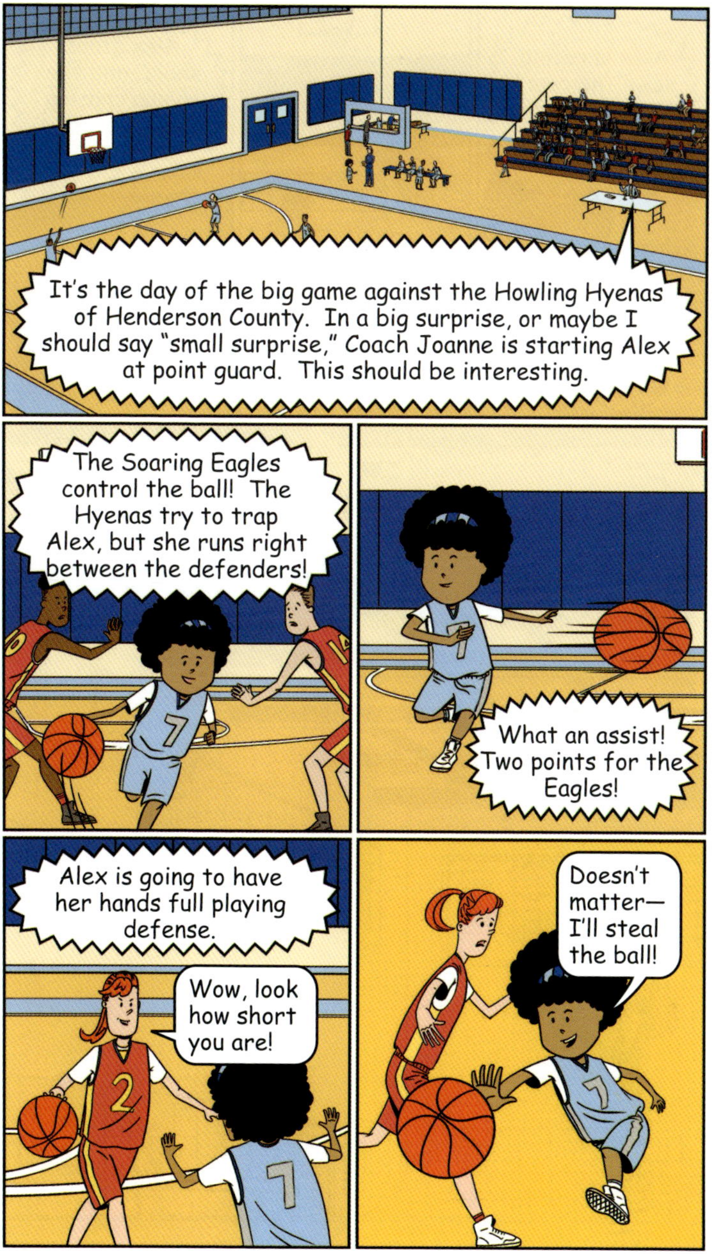
It's the day of the big game against the Howling Hyenas of Henderson County. In a big surprise, or maybe I should say "small surprise," Coach Joanne is starting Alex at point guard. This should be interesting.
The Soaring Eagles control the ball! The Hyenas try to trap Alex, but she runs right between the defenders!
What an assist! Two points for the Eagles!
Alex is going to have her hands full playing defense.
Wow, look how short you are!
Doesn't matter— I'll steal the ball!

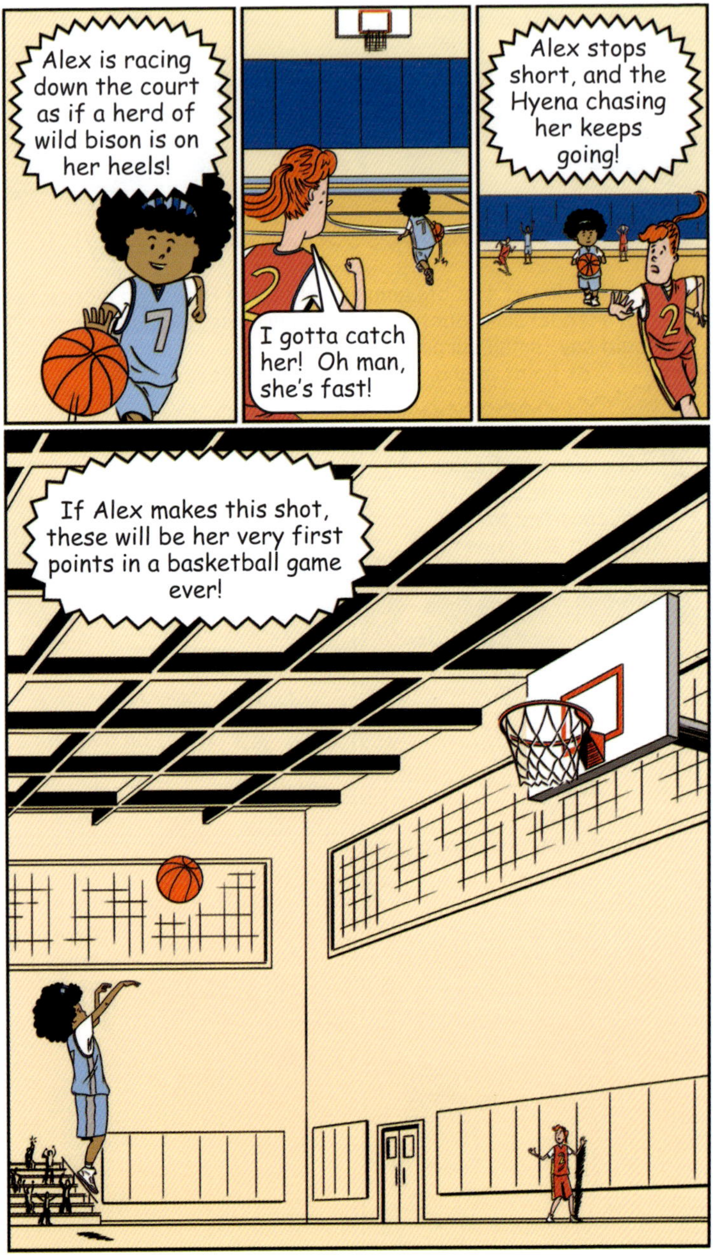
Alex is racing down the court as if a herd of wild bison is on her heels!
I gotta catch her! Oh man, she's fast!
Alex stops short, and the Hyena chasing her keeps going!
If Alex makes this shot, these will be her very first points in a basketball game ever!

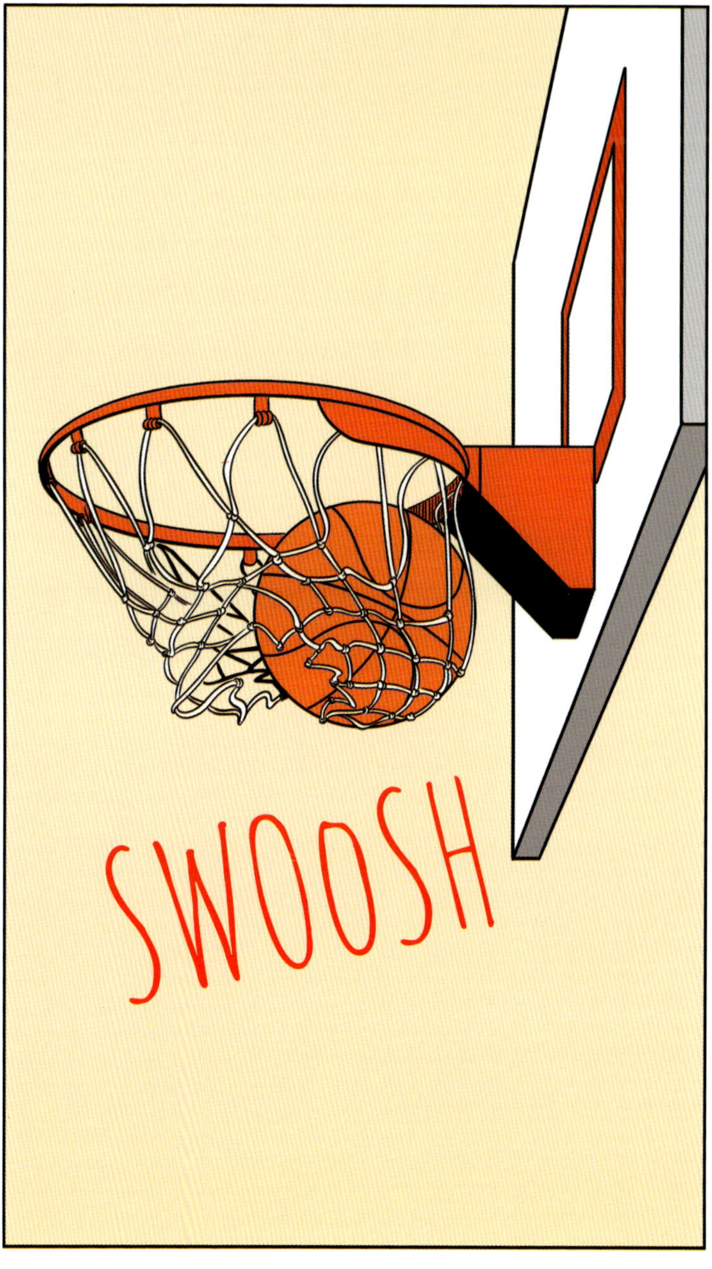
SWOOSH

About Us

The Author

Joe Rhatigan is an author and book editor who lives in Asheville, North Carolina, with his family and his dog named Rooster. He started out as a tall basketball player, but then everyone caught up to him!

The Illustrator

Joseph McDermott remembers drawing the panels from his comic books and creating scenes featuring his favorite cartoon characters when he was a boy growing up in New Jersey. Now based in Philadelphia, he's doing the same thing as a career. Joseph has trained in drawing, painting, sculpture, screen-printing, typography, and photography. He has a Scottish terrier named Monty and a large collection of vinyl albums, and he still loves his comics.